Pop's Old Car

By Annette Smith
Illustrations by Anne Spudv

My pop has an old car.

It is very, very old.

One of Pop's friends
gave him the old car a long time ago.

Pop's friend didn't want it any more.

The old car was broken down.

It had mud all over the wheels
and the doors and the roof.

There was grass growing under the seats.

Some spiders had made big webs
around the windows.

But my pop is very clever.

He can fix cars.

Now the old car looks so good.
Pop keeps it in a shed
behind the garage.

There is a big lock
on the door of the shed.

Pop put it there
so that his car will be safe.

No one can go into the shed
without Pop.

He has the key for the lock.

The outside of the car is black.

The seats inside the car are white.

The car has two big lights at the front, and two little red lights at the back.

The wheels on the car have small black tyres and long black **spokes**.

Every Saturday morning,
Pop cleans his old car.

He puts some soap and warm water
in a bucket.

First, he washes the windows
and the doors.

Then, he cleans the wheels with a brush.

He is very careful
when he cleans around the big lights.

Pop always looks at the **engine** and the brakes
before he takes the car out on the road.
He does not want the car to stop
or have an accident.

Pop never drives the car in the **city**.
He likes to drive it out in the country.
The old car cannot go very fast up hills.

Pop has a new big car in the garage
by the shed.

The new car can go much faster
than the old car.

But Pop still likes his little old car the best.

1927

Glossary

city a very big town

engine a machine that makes things move

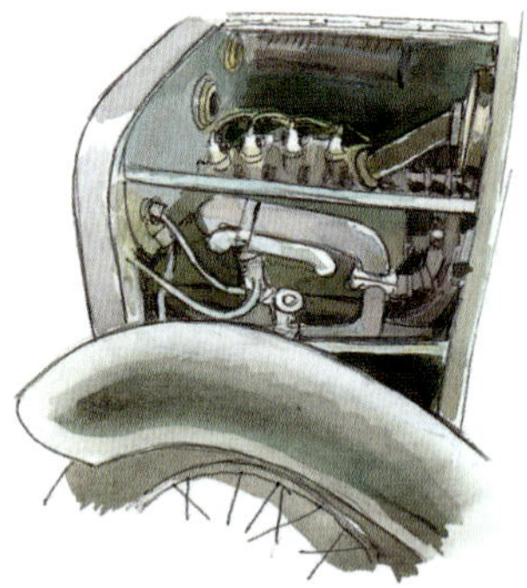

spokes the rods inside a wheel

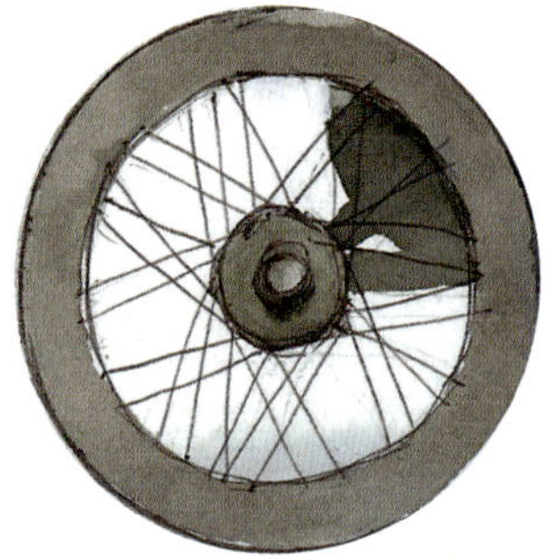